JENN

summer
LAKE

SADDLEBACK
EDUCATIONAL PUBLISHING

MONARCH
JUNGLE

SADDLEBACK
EDUCATIONAL PUBLISHING
www.sdlback.com

ISBN-13: 978-1-68021-480-2
ISBN-10: 1-68021-480-2
eBook: 978-1-63078-834-6

Printed in Guangzhou, China
NOR/0118/CA21800081

22 21 20 19 18   1 2 3 4 5

MONARCH
JUNGLE

The Big Idea

Hey, Rayna," Cora said. "Can you hand me the popcorn?"

Cora was on her bed reading. Rayna was sitting on the floor. She was staring at her phone. A few seconds of silence went by.

"Rayna! Popcorn?"

"What? Oh, sorry. Here you go." She handed the bowl to Cora.

"Don't you have homework?"

"Yeah," Rayna said. "I'm just reading a story on Twitter. Listen to this. Some guys were hiking. They found an old trunk. There were gold coins inside."

"Like buried treasure? That's so cool," Cora said. "Where were they hiking?"

"Near a dried-up river."

"Did the coins belong to pirates?" Cora laughed.

"Not quite," Rayna said. "It just says the trunk is about 100 years old. If the river had water, it wouldn't have been found."

"The drought is good for something, I guess."

The girls lived in the foothills. There were miles of land around them. There used to be so much green. Now everything was brown and dry. There had been many wildfires.

This was the third year of a drought. There was little water. The town had set limits on using it. That meant taking short showers. People couldn't water their lawns or fill their pools.

"Do you think there's more treasure?" Cora asked. "There are so many dried-up places. Like—"

Before she could finish, Rayna had jumped up. The girls were looking at each other.

"Summer Lake!" they called out.

"Let's talk to Lucas," Cora said. "He may know about this."

Lucas was Cora's older brother. Camping was his hobby. Every chance he got, he'd head for the lake. It made him feel close to their dad. He'd died a few years ago.

He taught Lucas all the basics. What gear to pack. How to set up a tent and make a fire. Mostly how to be safe in nature.

Now Lucas was the one to take his sister camping. He'd taught her all the same things. On these trips, they'd fish and hike. Cora really loved to hike.

One time Rayna went with them. At first she hated to be away from her phone. But she started to love being outdoors. It was good exercise. And the photos were great for social media.

After that trip, the girls set a goal. They would hike the Pacific Crest Trail. Not the whole thing. Just a portion. The entire PCT stretched from Mexico to Canada.

They planned to go after graduating high school. That was still three years away. But hiking to the lake would be good practice.

Rayna was reading again. "Part of Summer Lake is dried up," she said.

"Which part?" Cora asked.

"The eastern region, it says here. I'll pull up a map of the area."

"Here," Cora said. She pulled a box out from under her bed. Inside were a stack of paper maps.

"Not those maps. I mean a map app."

"Too late." Cora had a map spread out on the bed.

Rayna rolled her eyes. "I can't believe we're friends."

"What do you think we'll use on a hike?" Cora said. "An app won't help us if we can't get a signal." She pointed to a spot on the map. "There it is. Summer Lake. Doesn't it look amazing?"

"Oh sure," Rayna said. "If you think the world is flat."

"Whatever. Let's go see if Lucas is home."

Chapter 2

Good to Go

Cora and Rayna were on their way down the hall. The front door opened. Cora's mom stepped inside. There were two bags of groceries in her arms.

"Perfect timing," she said. "Can you help me, Cora? There are two pizzas in the car."

"Sure. Be right back."

"Hi, Rayna," Mrs. Evans said. "Can you stay for dinner? We have plenty of food." She put the bags down. "I just need to get plates."

Cora came in carrying the pizzas. Lucas was behind her. He'd been out jogging. They all sat down at the table.

"It was a long day," Mrs. Evans said.

"Here it comes," Lucas said.

Mrs. Evans was an ER nurse. Most of her stories had gory details.

"One man had pieces of glass in his eyes. Another man had a knife stuck—"

"Mom!" Cora said. "Stop! We're eating."

"I have some good news," Lucas said. "You know the wildlife center? I might get a summer job there. They need a lab assistant. My science teacher put in a good word for me."

"That's perfect for you," Mrs. Evans said.

"Right? Last year they rescued a condor. Not many people get to see one up close."

Lucas was starting college in the fall. Ever since middle school, he planned to major in science. After high school, he wanted to work with wild animals.

"Does anyone else have news?" Mrs. Evans asked. "Cora? Rayna?"

The girls looked at each other and smiled.

"Uh-oh," Lucas said. "This could mean trouble. What are you guys up to?"

Cora told them the whole story. How gold coins were found in a dried-up riverbed. "We want to search the area around Summer Lake," she said. "Can you take us, Lucas? Please?"

"Those trails aren't exactly easy," Mrs. Evans said. "And what about wildfires?"

"We'd be with Lucas," Cora said. "He would keep us safe. And it will be good training for the PCT."

"How do you know he'll take you? Not only that, your trip is a long way off. You won't be 18 for another three years. Isn't it early to start training?"

"Actually, no," Lucas said. "They're serious about the PCT. So they should hike as much as they can. It will help them get ready. I'll take them over spring break. If it's okay with Rayna's parents."

Cora jumped up. "Yes! That's in two weeks! Come on, Rayna. Let's start planning."

"Hold on," Lucas said. "I want to warn you. You probably won't find treasure. And even if there were some? That Twitter story was seen by a lot of people. They could have the same idea."

The girls were halfway down the hall.

"Do you think he's right?" Rayna asked. "We won't find any treasure?"

"He's just trying to spoil the fun. As usual."

Chapter 3

It's a Plan!

Cora loved to make plans. It didn't matter what she was doing. A school day was as important as a vacation. There were always a few handwritten lists. Not being prepared could ruin everything.

The hiking trip was no different. There were so many details to work out. What gear did they have? What was still needed? What supplies would they take?

Lucas was a big help. He knew everything about camping. Like how much water to take. As warm and dry as it was, they would need a lot. It would make their packs heavy. That meant taking less of something else.

Food was tricky, he'd said. During a normal year, they could cook over a fire. But with the drought, that was too risky. Wildfires were a real danger.

They would have to take prepackaged foods. Things like meal bars were perfect, Cora decided.

She also did research. The best trails to take. The best spots to camp. The dos and don'ts of hiking.

Planning was important. But it also helped the time go by. Cora couldn't wait for the trip. Now if only school would end.

The two weeks seemed to drag. Today was the worst. It was Friday, and social studies was so boring.

Mr. Cortez was talking about the United Nations. But Cora hadn't been listening. Her mind was on the supply list.

Sleeping bags. Check.

Tents. Check.

Sun hats. Check.

Shovel. Ch—

"Cora?" Mr. Cortez said. "Are you listening?"

"What?" Cora said, looking up. Everyone was staring at her. "Sorry. I didn't hear you."

"I'll repeat the question. What is the purpose of the UN?"

"To unite nations?"

Everyone laughed.

"Quick thinking. Imagine what you'd learn if you paid attention."

The bell rang. Cora packed up her things. She hurried out the door. Rayna was waiting outside the building.

"I made you a to-do list," Cora said. "Do you mind?" She knew that Rayna wasn't a big planner. "It won't take long. It's mostly research so we know what to expect."

If it were up to Rayna, she'd rather be surprised. But she took the list. Doing research wasn't that bad. At least she'd be online. She was never far from her phone or social media.

Chapter 4

Warning Signs

Rayna sat on her bed. She'd just posted a selfie. It showed her in sunglasses and holding a backpack. There was a caption. "Glamping trip coming up! #lookinggood."

She glanced over at her desk. The to-do list had been sitting there. It wasn't going away. *Fine!* She gave in and grabbed it.

"Things to research. Snake bites. Poison oak. High and low temperatures. Animals in the area."

She typed *snake* in the search box. Then her phone buzzed. It was a text from Cora.

"Can U go 2 Great Gear? Get meal bars, trail mix, beef jerky. TY!"

"OK," Rayna texted. "Will call U when I'm back." She looked up and saw her mom at the door.

"I'm going to run some errands. Need anything?"

"Can you take me to Great Gear?"

"Sure. But let's go now. Before the bank closes."

Rayna's mom stopped in front of Great Gear. "Is 20 minutes enough time?" she asked.

"Should be. Thanks, Mom." She got out of the car.

Her mom waved and drove off.

As Rayna walked to the door, someone started laughing. It was coming from a group of boys.

There was something about the looks on their faces. It made her nervous. She hurried inside.

First on the list was meal bars. A clerk handed her a basket. Then he led her to the food aisle. The shelves were filled with packages. Most foods were freeze-dried. Some looked really good. Like Thai peanut noodles. But Cora said to keep it simple.

Rayna grabbed a box of meal bars. Just then someone laughed. She looked over. It was two of the boys from outside.

"Going camping?" one of them asked.

Her first thought was to drop the basket and go. But then the boys left. The checkout counter was just steps away. It would take only a few minutes more. By then, her mom would be back.

"Find what you need?" a clerk asked.

"Yes." Rayna looked around. "But I'm kind of in a hurry."

"Sure." He gave her the total.

She paid and walked away.

"Your receipt," the clerk called.

In her rush to leave, Rayna hadn't heard him.

Chapter 5

Haters

Rayna's fears were coming true. The boys were outside. They stood side by side, forming a wall. It seemed they were waiting for her. No words were spoken. But their eyes were cold.

"Excuse me," she said. "Can I get through, please?" But the boys didn't move. Where was her mother?

"You're not going anywhere," one of them said. He took a step toward her.

Rayna looked at him. "What?"

"We know about you," he said. Now his arms were crossed. The other boys were staring at her.

"What are you talking about?" Rayna asked.

"You, terrorist."

"Me?" she said. Her heart was pounding. "That's crazy."

"You're not American," another boy said.

"My family is from India. But I'm American. We probably go to the same school."

Rayna looked around. A few people had stopped to watch. "Can someone help me?" she asked.

No one spoke. A woman holding a child hurried away.

"Who wants to help a terrorist?" the boy said. He stepped closer to Rayna.

"Back off," someone said.

Rayna stood frozen. Then she felt a hand on her shoulder. A woman was standing next to her.

"It's okay," the woman said.

By now the boys had started shouting. The woman's grip on Rayna tightened. She felt herself being moved along. They were going back into Great Gear.

As the door closed behind them, the shouting faded. But the boys looked in through the window. Some shook their fists.

"Those guys are jerks," the woman said. "You're shaking. Are you okay?"

"I'm not sure," Rayna said. "My mom should be here by now." She looked out the window. Her mom had pulled up to the curb. "Would you mind—"

"No problem," the woman said. "Ready to make a run for it?"

Rayna nodded. The woman took her by the arm. Then the two ran from the store. They stopped at the car.

"Thank you," Rayna said. Then she opened the door and got in. The door slammed behind her.

"What's going on?" her mom asked. "Who was that woman?"

Tears ran down Rayna's face.

"Oh, honey. What's wrong?"

There was no way to explain this. Her parents would not understand. First they would call the police. And then Rayna would never be allowed to leave the house alone.

"Please, Mom. Let's just go."

On the way home, her mom kept asking questions.

"What's wrong?"

"What happened?"

"Are you okay?"

All Rayna could do was shake her head. When they got to the house, she ran inside. She locked her bedroom door behind her.

After a few minutes, she heard voices outside the door. Her parents and grandmother were talking.

"What is wrong with her?" Rayna's dad asked.

"I'm not sure," her mom said.

Then there was a knock on her door.

"Are you sick?" her mom asked. "Did something happen at the store? Is it school?"

"Talk to us," her dad said. "Let us help you."

"Please leave me alone," Rayna said.

There was silence. Then she heard her grandmother say, "This isn't helping. Let's give her some time."

Chapter 6

What's the Problem?

It was 6:00 p.m. Cora checked her phone. Rayna hadn't called or texted. She was supposed to call after shopping. That was two hours ago. As Cora started a text, her phone buzzed. It was Rayna's mom calling.

"Have you heard from Rayna?" she asked.

"I haven't. Is everything okay?"

"I don't think so. She hasn't left her room. She won't talk to us. Can you come over? Maybe she'll tell you what's wrong."

"I'll be right there," Cora said. Before she left, she called Rayna. There was no answer.

"Mom," she called on her way to the front door. "I need to go to Rayna's. She's really upset about something."

"Okay. Call me if you need anything."

It was a short walk to Rayna's house. She lived just down the block. The door opened before Cora could knock.

"Thank you for coming," Rayna's mom said. "I'm so worried. I've never seen my daughter like this."

"I'll talk to her," Cora said. She went to Rayna's door and knocked. Then she knocked again. "It's just me. Can I come in?"

The door opened. Rayna stood there. Her eyes were red from crying.

"What's wrong, Rayna?"

"Quick. Come in. And close the door."

Cora closed the door behind her. The girls sat on the bed.

"You can't tell my parents," Rayna said.

"I won't."

"There were these boys at the store. They were following me around and laughing. When I went outside, they blocked my way. One of them called me a terrorist."

"Why?" Cora asked.

"How would I know? Maybe because I have dark skin?" Rayna's voice was rising. "Because they're stupid?"

Cora stared at Rayna. Then she started laughing.

Rayna jumped up. "What? Why are you laughing? What's so funny?"

"You're joking, right?" Cora asked.

"No! I'm not joking! Do I look like I'm joking?"

"Okay! Okay!" Cora said. "I think you need to calm down."

Rayna began to shake. Her face was red with anger. "Calm down?" Her voice had gotten louder.

"Yeah. I'm sorry you're upset. But it's over. You'll be okay. Let's talk about the trip. Did you get the food?"

"Get out!" Rayna cried. "And take your stupid food with you!"

"Why? What did I—"

"Just leave! Now!"

Cora grabbed the Great Gear bag and left. When she got home, she slammed the door behind her.

"Hey!" Lucas said. He was sitting on the couch. "I'm trying to read."

"You're studying? Seriously?" Cora said. "You're almost done with high school."

"You've heard of finals?"

She sat down on the couch. "You're in a bad mood too?"

"Not me," he said without looking up. "It sounds like you are, though."

"It's Rayna. I was just at her house. You should have seen her. She got really mad and kicked me out!"

"Why?"

"There were some boys at Great Gear. She said they were laughing at her. It freaked her out."

"There had to be more to it than just laughing."

"She said they called her a terrorist."

Chapter 7

No Joke

They called Rayna a terrorist?" Lucas asked. "That sounds serious, Cora."

"People say all kinds of crazy things. Rayna should know from being online. You can't take it personally."

"Wow. Really?" Lucas said. "You don't think calling someone a terrorist is bad? You need to pay more attention. Bad things happen in the world. Really bad things. It's not like the dream world you live in."

"Okay. I guess I messed up. What should I do? Go back over there?"

Lucas closed his book. "I don't know. You figure it out. Maybe start by being a better friend."

Cora stood up. "Hey! Don't say that. I *am* a good friend."

"You created a problem when there shouldn't be one. Some people have real problems, you know."

"Are you saying that you have problems? You, Mr. Perfect? That's what Mom tells everyone. Everything works out for you. A perfect summer job. The best college. A great girlfriend who—"

"Stop," Lucas said.

"What? Is it about Lena?"

"I can't tell you."

"Why not?"

"Because," Lucas said. "No one can know right now. Especially Mom."

"You can trust me. I won't say a word."

Lucas just sat there with his head hanging down. Cora had never seen him like this before. Finally he took a deep breath and looked at her.

"Lena might be pregnant," he said.

Cora's eyes got wide. "Oh no."

"Tell me about it."

"But you said 'might be.' She hasn't taken a test?"

"It's too soon," Lucas said. "Or she's too scared to take one."

"Have the two of you talked about it?"

"Lena would want to keep the baby."

"Will you guys get married?" Cora asked.

"It all just happened. So I don't even know. All I'm thinking is how my plans will change."

"Yeah. Just like Mom. When she got pregnant with you in high school. This is exactly what she didn't want to happen."

"I know," Lucas said. "I'm scared."

"Of what Mom will say? Or about the baby?"

"Both."

"Mom is going to freak."

"Just don't tell her," Lucas said.

"I won't." Cora went into her bedroom. She picked up her phone and texted Rayna. "Need to talk to you. Please text me." There was no answer. After a few minutes, she tried again. Still, there was no reply.

It was hard to focus on anything the rest of the night. Rayna had been mad at her before. But never for this long.

When it was time for bed, she kept her phone close. Maybe she would get a text.

In the morning, Cora checked for messages. There weren't any. As she was getting dressed, there was a knock on her door.

"Get out here," Lucas called. "You have to see this."

"See what?" she called back.

"Just hurry."

"Okay! I'm coming!" Cora stopped outside Lucas's bedroom door. He was on his laptop. "What's so important?"

"Have you talked to Rayna?" he asked.

"No. She won't text me back."

"Come and watch this video," he said.

As Cora came up behind him, he hit play. There was the scene of a crowd. Some boys had formed a line. Their backs were to the camera. The person filming then walked around. Now their faces were in the shot.

"That makes you a terrorist," one of them said.

The camera panned and stopped. Cora gasped. It was Rayna! She was shaking. Her eyes were wide with fear. Cora had never seen anyone look so scared.

"Can someone help me?" Rayna asked.

A woman put a hand on Rayna's shoulder and led her away. That was the end of the video.

Lucas looked up from the screen. "This was serious," he said. "Did you see how scared Rayna was? Everyone was watching. And no one did anything. Rayna really needed you. You messed up, Cora."

Cora started to cry. She thought back to the day before. Why hadn't she been a better friend? Would Rayna ever forgive her?

Chapter 8

It's Not Okay

Rayna woke up late Saturday morning. For a second, she thought she'd had a bad dream. Bullies hadn't really attacked her. But then she remembered. It did happen.

She looked at her phone. There were many texts from Cora. *Some best friend*, Rayna thought. What those bullies did was bad enough. But it could have been much worse. Hate crimes were real. She expected Cora to get that.

Now it was too late. Rayna didn't want to see or talk to her. She'd even turned off her phone. That was after Cora started blowing it up. In the latest text, she seemed really upset.

"I need to talk to you. Please text me. Or call. You can yell at me. Just give me a chance. Please!"

Part of Rayna wanted to text Cora. But mostly she just wanted to forget about the whole thing.

Then she went downstairs. Her family was gathered around a computer. Her mom and grandmother were crying.

"What's wrong?" Rayna asked.

Her dad stood and put his arms around her. "My poor child," he said. "You should have told us."

He stepped aside. A video was playing on the screen. It was the boys bullying her. Someone had filmed it.

"I didn't want you to be scared," Rayna said.

"We're your parents," her dad said. "It's our job to protect you."

"You couldn't have done anything," she said.

"Sit down," Rayna's grandmother said. "I'll make some tea."

Rayna sat with her family. She told them the entire story.

After they talked and drank tea, Rayna went to her room. She opened the video on her phone. A few of the comments surprised her. They were mean.

"You're not one of us."

"Go back where you came from."

But most people stood up for Rayna.

"This girl is so brave."

"Fight hate!"

"People like these are cowards."

Rayna read the comments over and over. People were telling her that the boys were wrong. They had no right to bully her. All people had a place in their town.

She wiped tears from her face. These tears weren't from fear or even sadness. Rayna felt anger. It was like she had found something to fight for.

Chapter 9

Change of Plans

On Monday, Cora got to school early. She waited in the parking lot for Rayna. The two would talk. Everything would be okay. That was the plan anyway.

Today Rayna's dad dropped her off. As soon as he left, Cora hurried over to her.

"I'm so sorry for the way I acted. I was a jerk," Cora said. "You needed a friend. And I didn't listen. Now I understand."

Rayna stood there in silence as Cora went on.

"At first I didn't get it. But now I do. If someone was mean to me, you'd be upset. You would have been there for me."

"Okay!" Rayna said. "It's okay. I'm not mad at you anymore."

Rayna opened her arms. Cora leaned into her. The

girls hugged. Then Cora pulled away. She gripped Rayna's arms and stepped back. "How are you? Have your parents seen the video?"

"They know," Rayna said. "I'm actually glad. It feels good to be able to talk to them. I don't want to have secrets."

"Have those boys bothered you again?"

"No," Rayna said. "I've thought about it. They're a bunch of bullies. But I don't think they planned to come after me. I was just there. And I happened to have brown skin. I was an easy target."

"I think they're monsters," Cora said.

"One thing you said was right. It's over. And I'll be okay."

Cora looked down and shook her head. "Yeah, but I should have taken it more seriously. If something like that happened to me—"

"I would have kicked their butts."

Just then the bell rang.

"Let's get to class," Rayna said.

The two headed for the entrance.

"So I'll see you at lunch?" Cora said. "We can talk about Summer Lake. It's going to be so much fun. I can't wait."

Rayna shook her head. "I can't go," she said. "I need to be near my family."

"You're right. We should wait until you're feeling better. This summer."

The girls stopped and looked at each other.

"No, Cora. You're not hearing me. I don't want to go at all. Not now. Not this summer. Not ever."

The second bell rang.

"We *have* to go," Cora said. She could feel herself getting mad. Her voice was shaking. "We've put so much work into planning the trip! How can you back out now?"

"How can I?" Rayna said. "Because there are way more important things to do. And think about. There are problems in the world. Real problems. I want to help solve them. Not run off to search for imaginary treasure."

"But you were so excited."

"Things change," Rayna said. "Maybe I've changed."

Tears came to Cora's eyes. She started to cry.

"I'm late for class," Rayna said. Then she turned and walked away.

Cora just stood there and watched her.

Chapter 10

Last Hope

What just happened? Cora thought. She'd wanted to fix things with Rayna. And she had. Until she brought up Summer Lake.

The two of them had always been so close. Nothing kept them apart. Not even an argument. Now it seemed like their friendship was ending. Or maybe Rayna just needed space. She'd think about it and change her mind.

For now, Cora and Lucas would go. It would be a great trip. Cora would come home with stories for Rayna. Rayna would see what she'd missed out on. She would go next time.

At lunch she went to find Rayna. They always sat at the same table. Today no one was there. Instead, Rayna was sitting with another friend. Again, Cora felt like crying. But this time, she held back the tears.

Now she went to Lucas's lunch spot. It was a bench by the library. "I need to talk to you," she said.

"What's going on?" he asked.

"I told Rayna how sorry I am. And we talked. But now she doesn't want to go to Summer Lake. She thinks it's a waste of time."

Lucas put his arm around Cora. "I'm sorry," he said.

"You're still going with me. Right?"

Lucas didn't say anything.

"What?" she said. "No. Don't tell me—"

"I can't go, Cora. Not with everything that's going on. With Lena maybe ..."

Cora's heart was pounding. She felt her face getting hot. How could everyone let her down like this? "You are so selfish," she said.

Lucas stood up. "*I'm* selfish? Look who's talking. Lena and I are going through a really tough time. Your best friend was attacked by bullies. And all you can think about is your stupid trip. You need to grow up."

Lucas's words hurt. They made Cora feel foolish. Like she didn't have a clue about life.

"Well, I'm going to Summer Lake," she said. "Even if you won't go with me."

Lucas laughed. "Come on. Mom won't let you go alone. There's no way."

Cora's mind raced. There had to be a way she could still go.

"Mom won't know," she said. "Because you're going to lie for me."

"No, I'm not," he said. He turned and started to walk away. "That's crazy."

"You will lie," Cora said. Her heart pounded harder. She knew that she might regret what she was about to say. But it was the only way.

"You will lie for me," she said. "Or I'll tell Mom about Lena."

Lucas spun around. At first he looked angry. "You wouldn't do that," he said. Then his face changed. He looked sad.

Cora couldn't look him in the eyes. "I will," she said. "I'll tell Mom if you don't help me."

Lucas shook his head. "That's pretty low." Then he turned and walked away.

Chapter 11

No Turning Back

It was Saturday morning. Cora had been up since sunrise. She'd packed her small items the night before.

Now, with checklist in hand, she sorted her gear. Map and compass. Tent and sleeping bag. Knife, flashlight, first-aid kit. Food and water. Digital camera.

Everything was in her pack. It was time to go. There was just one last thing. She started a text to Rayna. Then something made her stop.

The girls hadn't spoken since their fight. Rayna was probably still mad. She needed more time. It was best to leave her alone.

On her way down the hall, she heard the TV. Lucas was in the living room. Part of her wanted to sneak out. But now she was curious. Had he changed his mind? Maybe he was packed and ready to go.

She walked into the room. Her brother didn't look up. "I'm going," she said.

He just stared at the screen. Cora wished he would hug her. Or say good luck.

For a second, she thought about staying home. Hiking alone wasn't the best idea. But it was too late to admit that now and back out.

Cora left the house and walked to the bus stop. As she waited, she thought about what she was doing. *What if I get lost? What if there's a wildfire?* Her best friend and her brother were angry. She was lying to her mom.

The bus pulled up and the door opened. Cora just stood there.

"Are you coming?" the driver asked.

Cora got on the bus and paid the fare. When she sat down, she got out her phone. She texted Rayna. "I'm leaving now for Summer Lake. Alone. I'll be thinking of you the whole time. I'll miss you."

She pressed send. Then she turned off her phone. She wouldn't need it.

Chapter 12

Going, Going, Gone

The bus ride took two hours. That gave Cora a lot of time to think. Lucas's words had hurt her. Did he really think she was selfish? She loved her brother so much. Having his approval meant everything.

Finally the bus stopped and Cora got off. Ahead was a visitor's lot. She'd been to this spot before. Normally there were a lot of cars. Families liked to camp here. Now the place seemed empty. For a day trip, that would be good. But for an overnight trip, it was a little scary.

You're safe, she told herself. *You can do this.*

Cora took a deep breath. The air felt different here. It was fresh and clean. She put her pack on and headed off.

At first the pack felt heavy on her back. She started to sweat. Her shirt stuck to the pack. The dirt on the trail was loose and dry. After an hour of hiking, dust covered her boots and socks. Dust filled her nose and got in her eyes.

An oak tree was ahead. It gave off some shade. Cora stopped to rest. She took a long drink of water and looked around.

Even though it was spring, nothing was green. There were no flowers. Most of the trees looked dead. The brown weeds were dry. The smallest spark could set them on fire.

The cool air had turned warm. She put on her hat and started walking again. Soon she forgot about the weight of the pack. Now it seemed like it was part of her body.

In the stillness, thoughts began to fill her mind. First of Rayna. Then of Lucas and her mom. She thought about everything that had happened. Would she and Rayna be friends again? Cora forced herself to think about something else.

What would her life be like? She loved high school. But college? It would only lead to a boring office job. No amount of money would make that okay.

Being tested mattered more. Mentally and physically. That's what hiking did for her. She could see herself traveling too. Hiking in other countries. Maybe with a partner someday.

She knew what her mom would say. Find a job that fits her interests. Something like the Peace Corps.

Rayna came to mind again. Cora could see her having a perfect life. Married. One or two children. Living in a nice house.

Nothing was wrong with that. Unless it was only about image. And none of it really made you happy.

Cora thought of Rayna's selfies. Posing in camping clothes. Her perfect hair and makeup. Come on!

Wow! Cora thought. She'd never let herself think this way. *It must be the heat.*

"I'm going crazy!" she called out. Then she looked around. How funny it would be if someone had heard that. A rabbit leaped across the trail. Cora laughed.

What other animals would she see? Rayna was supposed to find out. But that never happened.

Cora stopped and looked up. A hawk soared overhead. She watched it make slow, wide circles in the sky. It was like a graceful dance.

There was no way to know what the bird was thinking. But it seemed happy.

Chapter 13

Dream World

Cora was filled with hope. Something waited for her at Summer Lake. Maybe not treasure. But something special.

As she walked, she felt a rush of good feelings. There was beauty in everything she saw. The oak trees with their tangled roots. The way the branches cast shadows across the trail. Even the creepy-looking turkey vultures.

This is why she loved hiking. Any problems she had were small. There was more to life.

Then she remembered the camera. It was in her shirt pocket. The best parts of the trail were coming up. She wanted to get some pictures.

Her mind wandered to what was ahead. Her campsite. The sunset. Sleep. Then Summer Lake.

What if she did find treasure? Lucas and Rayna would die of shock.

Suddenly Cora felt herself slip. Her ankle twisted. She'd stepped on a loose stone. Now she could see that the whole trail was stones. This was a creek bed.

How long had she been off the trail? When she looked back, it wasn't even in sight.

It's okay, she thought. *Just turn around. Go back the way you came.* But part of her was scared. What if she couldn't find her way back?

Now it was early afternoon. The sun beat down. Without a breeze, the air was heavy. It made it hard to breathe.

Cora's mouth was dry. She took a sip of water. Then she took out her map. Her finger traced the trail. Off to one side was Berry Creek. That had to be where she was. The trail was west of there.

Easy enough. Just head west back to the trail.

Cora looked at her compass. She started walking. A voice in her head said she was lost. But she tried to ignore it. Maps didn't lie. All she had to do was trust herself and keep walking.

Up ahead, the path seemed to end. Plants covered the trail. Their leaves were in groups of three. They had pointed tips. Poison oak! Brushing against it could cause a painful rash.

She took out the map again. There was only one path

to the trail. It was through the poison oak. Going around it would just get her lost again.

Cora's mind raced. What if she was wrong? If Rayna was there, they would decide together. If Lucas was there, they wouldn't have gotten lost at all. But she was alone. It was up to her.

She'd come too far. The heat hadn't killed her. A little poison oak wouldn't either. The worst that could happen was to get a bad rash. She could deal with that. Right now, the important thing was to find the trail.

She tried to walk quickly. But this was more than a little poison oak. The area was thick with shrubs and vines. With each step, her pants brushed against the leaves.

Cora was so focused on the ground that she almost missed the trail. But then she saw the dirt path. Tears filled her eyes. She didn't realize how scared she'd been.

This was a good time to take a break. She walked to the nearest tree and let the pack drop. It felt good to be free of the weight. Then she ate a meal bar and drank some water. She would need her energy.

The next part of the trail was tricky. It was steeper, and it took a lot of turns. She would really need to focus.

Chapter 14

Meltdown

This was the hottest part of the day. Cora's energy was low. And it was another five miles to the campsite.

Every few minutes, she took a sip of water. That made her worry. *What if the water runs out? What if I faint? Why am I here by myself?*

"Stop it!" she said out loud. But the negative thoughts kept coming. And she was too tired to fight them.

A flood of images filled her head. First it was Lucas shouting at her. Then she saw Rayna in the video. Those bullies made Cora sick.

People hating others for looking different? Was the world really that bad? Lucas said it was. Cora should have known. But she didn't go online that much. She didn't watch the news. Most of the time, she was reading a book.

Rayna was online a lot. Checking her status. Posting selfies. She shared so much of her life. People had to be careful. Especially with the haters in the world.

Maybe she shouldn't share so much. But that didn't make sense either. People should be free to express themselves.

The straps of Cora's pack dug into her back. As the trail climbed, her pace got quicker. It was like the pain was pushing her.

She thought about this hike. How Rayna backed out. The way Cora acted was childish. Telling Rayna that she had to go. But she didn't mean to hurt her friend. It was just such a letdown. The two wouldn't share this adventure. Why didn't Rayna get that?

Cora stopped. Her thoughts were so loud in her head. She stood still and listened. There was only silence.

The sun was blazing. Sweat dripped down her face. She looked up at the sky. Everything was still. There wasn't a single bird in sight. Anything alive was hiding in some hidden shady spot.

She took a deep breath and walked on. In a few hours, the sun would be setting. She needed to get to the campsite.

The trail continued to climb. But her legs were strong. And her mind was calm.

"I have to prove I can do this," she said. "To Lucas and Rayna. And to myself."

Suddenly she stopped. Something was on the trail. It was animal droppings. But what kind? Bear or deer? It mattered a lot.

If they belonged to a bear, that could mean trouble. Lucas had taught her how to tell. She leaned over for a closer look. Bear droppings!

In a normal year, bears wouldn't be here. But this was a drought. Animals were forced from their normal areas. They had to find water and food in other places.

Cora looked around. She felt like someone or something was watching her. But she continued on.

The trail wove through a grove of trees. She knew this place. A memory came to mind.

Lucas had taken Cora and Rayna camping. They set up their tents under these trees. Lucas made a fire.

After the sun had set, Cora told jokes. Rayna had laughed so hard. "Stop! You're going to make me pee!" she said.

She told more jokes. Rayna laughed even harder.

Cora smiled at the memory. She loved making Rayna laugh.

Then the three of them took turns telling scary stories. Rayna's were the best. They had creepy characters.

Masked strangers staring through windows. Serial killers hiding in closets. Crazed clowns stalking campers.

Just then there was a sound. Cora jumped. A chill went up her spine. When she looked around, nothing was there.

But then she heard the sound again. It was coming from behind some trees.

Deer, she thought. *It's just deer. Don't freak out.* Deer were common in these hills.

She looked carefully in the direction of the sound. Seeing a deer would make her feel better. But she didn't see anything.

"It can't be a bear," she said. But she knew what to do it if was. Lucas had told her many times. *Do not run!*

A second later there was another sound. This time it was louder. It was coming from behind her. Something was moving through the bushes.

Cora turned to look. There were four wild turkeys. They were walking in a line. She laughed. "Perfect," she said. "I feel like a turkey."

She took the camera from her pocket. "Smile, guys," she said as she took a picture.

Chapter 15

No Time to Cry

Seeing the turkeys had put Cora at ease. Maybe because they were a family. The thought reminded her of Lucas. Soon he would know she met her goal. She could exist safely in the wild. He would be proud of her.

Cora also thought of her mom. What would she think about this? Her baby being alone in the wild. She never would have agreed. Even though people had been doing it for all of human history. Now Cora knew she could do it too.

"I'm going to be okay," she said. Before, it was more of a question. Now, it was a statement. Saying it out loud made it true.

A breeze cooled her as she walked. The campsite wasn't much farther. There was one rocky section ahead.

Then she'd be there. She could eat and rest. The thought kept her going.

At first the rocks were small. They crunched under her boots. Soon they were more like boulders. Some had jagged edges. Pain shot through her feet.

She moved slowly, being careful to choose each step. One step on a loose rock and she'd fall.

The weight of her pack made it worse. It was hard to focus. *Take your time*, she thought.

As she took her next step, a rock moved. Then her foot slipped. There was nothing she could do. The pressure of the pack sent her forward. She landed hard on her hands and knees.

"No!" Cora rolled to one side. She undid the straps and slid out from her pack.

That's when she noticed her hands. Both palms were scraped. Then she felt pain. Her pants were torn over one knee. Ripped skin was showing. Blood was coming from a cut.

"It's okay," she said. "I just have to—" Cora was trying to stand. It took a minute to get up. As she stood there, her legs shook.

Scared to fall again, she didn't move. "Go!" she finally told herself.

The first step was painful. But she could walk. She pulled the first-aid kit from her pack and sat down.

As she pressed gauze to the cut, she felt a sting. Tears filled her eyes. "Do not cry!" Then she rinsed the cut and dried it. Last she applied a bandage.

After a few minutes, she put the kit away. Then she put on her pack and started walking.

As Cora moved past the rocky area, she could see the ridge. At last! It was her camping spot. The area was flat. Perfect for her tent.

Before setting up camp, she looked around. The ridge overlooked a small canyon. The river below was dry. Still, it was a nice view.

Cora took a few deep breaths. It felt good to be on solid ground. Even her knee was feeling better.

Now her feet were sore. She couldn't wait to take her boots off. And have something to eat.

First she set up the tent. Then she took a picture of it. It was proof of what she'd done. And without Rayna's help. Maybe she'd post it online so Rayna would see it. The thought made her sad.

There was no time for that. She'd worked too hard to get here. And the hardest part was still ahead.

Everything had to go just right. Not just physically. Her mind had to be clear.

She checked her supplies. There was plenty of water. And of course there was enough food. Rayna had bought enough for two.

That made Cora wonder. What was Rayna doing right now?

Think about something else! She'd been in such a rush to set up camp, she forgot about the poison oak. If she had a rash, she couldn't feel it.

She checked her arms and legs. No rash. And the cut on her knee had stopped bleeding. In a way, Cora was proud of it. It was like a badge she'd earned.

Chapter 16

You Are Not Alone

Cora sat outside the tent. It felt good to relax and not think about anything. All she'd done the whole day was think.

Her mood had changed so many times. From happy to sad and back to happy. Now her mind was calm. So was everything around her.

The sun was setting. Streaks of pink and red crossed the sky. A hawk swooped down into the canyon. The shadows were long. It was beautiful.

After a while, Cora went inside the tent. She crawled into her sleeping bag. "Summer Lake," she whispered. "It's really going to happen."

Her eyes closed. Just as she felt herself falling asleep, there was a noise. Bear? Turkeys? Deer? It didn't matter. Nothing mattered but sleep.

♕

"Huh?" Cora mumbled as she opened her eyes. She looked around. A sound had startled her awake. "What now?" She wasn't sure if it was night or day.

Then the sound got louder. She held her breath and listened. Was it footsteps? Her mind raced. It could be a hunter. Or another hiker. Maybe a park ranger, she hoped.

The footsteps were getting closer. Would the person stop? Why weren't they calling out?

Now her heart was pounding. Cora thought about the boys who bullied Rayna. People like that were full of hate. They could hurt you. Rayna said they'd asked her about camping. Had they come out here to find her?

Instead, they'd find Cora here alone. Who knew what they might do. Quietly she reached into her pack. She pulled out the knife. Her hand was shaking.

The footsteps kept getting closer.

"Hello?" a voice called.

Cora gripped the knife.

"Hello. Are you in there?"

Rayna? Cora put the knife down. She unzipped her tent and looked out. Rayna stood there smiling. She was wearing her pack. Sweat covered her face.

"Am I dreaming?" Cora said as she rubbed her eyes. "Is it really you?"

"It's me," Rayna said. "I'm really here."

"But how? Why?" By now she had climbed out of the tent. "I have so many questions. We have so much to talk about."

She went over to Rayna and gave her a hug. Her arms could barely reach around the pack. That's when Cora started to laugh. She had never been so happy to see anyone. Rayna laughed too.

"When I first saw you, I thought I'd lost my mind," Cora said. "Here, hand me your pack." She took the pack and set it down. "You must be tired."

"I could use something to eat," Rayna said. "Do you have any food?"

They looked at each other and laughed again. "Tons. Thanks to you. I'll get you something."

Cora went into the tent. She came back with two meal bars. The girls leaned against a boulder while Rayna ate.

"I can't believe you're here," Cora said. "You were so mad at me. What made you change your mind?"

"I read your text about coming here alone. Then I talked to Lucas. He said it was true. And that you were making him lie."

"Oh, that." Cora looked down. "It was wrong."

"I was so mad at you," Rayna said. "But then I thought about it. You're my best friend. I couldn't let you do this alone. What if something bad happened? I'd never forgive myself."

"But your parents. I can't believe they let you come. Especially after what those boys did."

"At first they said no. But I begged. Finally my grandma stood up for me. She said they should let me go. And they did."

"How did you get here so fast? You must have left right after me."

"It was a few hours later," Rayna said. "My dad drove me. Then I pushed myself to catch up to you."

"How did you know where—"

"The list of directions you left behind." She smiled at Cora. "You and your dumb lists."

Offline

You're such a good friend, Rayna. You always do the right thing. I don't deserve you," Cora said.

"You mean so much to me," Rayna said. "That's why I'm here. You know, Cora, I didn't handle things well either."

"What do you mean?"

"Those bullies upset me. And I took it out on you."

"But you were right to be mad. I was only thinking about the trip."

"You were just excited," Rayna said. "I should have told you how I felt. Instead, I blew up at you. You didn't deserve it."

"Thanks for saying that. I've been so worried about us. Our friendship. I didn't want to lose you."

"I have to admit something," Rayna said. "I think I share too much online. What those bullies did was wrong. There's no excuse. But maybe I made it easier for them."

"No. They're just haters. I've been thinking about something Lucas said. He told me that I need to go online more. To know what happens in the real world. I really didn't think people could be so hateful."

"That's funny," Rayna said.

Cora frowned. "What do you mean *funny*?"

"No. Not what you said. It's about me. I've been thinking about going online a lot less."

The girls sat in silence and gazed at the view. Bats flew up from the canyon. The stars were shining and the moon glowed.

Pretty soon they were too tired to keep their eyes open.

"Let's get some rest," Cora said. "Tomorrow is going to be a long day."

They settled into their sleeping bags. After a few minutes of talking, they were asleep.

"Rayna," Cora whispered. "Wake up."

Rayna opened her eyes. "What time is it?"

"It's almost five. We need to get going."

"I can't believe how well I slept," Rayna said.

"I've already eaten and packed up. Have something to eat. And I'll take the tent down."

Rayna quickly ate and packed her sleeping bag. Then, with packs on their backs, they left the area.

As they hiked, dust kicked up from their boots.

"We're almost there," Cora said. "Just a few more— Look! Down there!"

Rayna walked over and looked down. At the bottom of the slope was a riverbed. It looked like it had been carved into the land.

Instead of water, there were patches of scrub brush. Some portions were paved with boulders. There were a few pools of water. But it was brown and muddy or green and slimy.

They hiked down to the bottom of the slope.

"We made it," Cora said.

"It's so weird," Rayna said. "In a normal year, we'd be underwater right now."

They walked down into the riverbed. Cora saw an object and headed toward it. "Just an old shoe," she called back to Rayna. "And here's an old camp stove. Why would people dump their trash? It's disgusting."

"No. *This* is disgusting," Rayna said. "Beer cans and cigarette butts." She picked up a long stick and moved them aside. "It smells awful here. Like moldy food. Or dirty socks."

"Yuck," Cora said. Then she saw something. A deer and two fawns stood near a puddle. They were drinking the slimy water. "Over there," she said in a low voice. "Look!"

"Oh, they're so cute," Rayna said. "But look at that water. It's so gross. This must be all they have. How sad."

Chapter 18

Getting Real

I don't think we'll find anything," Cora said.

Rayna was poking around in the brush. "Don't give up yet. Hey! Look at this."

"You found something?" Cora ran over to her. "What is it?"

"I don't know. I'm trying to get it," Rayna said.

"Here. Let me try." Cora knelt down and grabbed the object. It was a small metal box. "It looks really old." She tried to open it, but the latch was rusted shut. "Quick. Hand me a rock."

Rayna found a rock and gave it to her.

"It could be treasure," Cora said. She struck the latch a few times.

"See?" Rayna said. "I told you not to give up. This is so exciting."

The latch finally broke off, and the box popped open. It was filled with mud. Cora shoveled it out with her hands. Suddenly she stopped.

"What?" Rayna said.

"There's nothing here. It's just mud." She wiped her hands on her pants. "I'm an idiot. I nearly ruined our friendship for nothing. I'm so sorry. You came all this way to dig through junk."

Rayna smiled. "It's okay," she said. Then she helped Cora up.

"Thanks, Rayna."

"For what?"

"You forgave me. And we're here together. Doing this stupid, wild, amazing thing. You hiked all this way just to dig through a slime pit. I must be the luckiest person alive. And I didn't even get a rash from the poison oak!"

"Or get eaten by a bear!" Rayna said.

"Or break my leg!"

"Only one thing could have made it better. We would have done the whole hike together," Rayna said. "And with Lucas."

Lucas, Cora thought. He was not going to be happy with her.

Rayna tossed the stick she was holding. "Do you want to leave?" she asked.

Cora nodded. They headed out of the riverbed and got their packs. At the top of the slope, they stopped and looked at each other.

"It's not too late," Rayna said. "We could go back."

Cora glanced down at the dried-up lake. "No thanks. I'm good."

She turned and walked to the trail. Rayna followed. Both girls were happy to leave Summer Lake.

The air was still cool. They walked at a quick pace. Soon the sun would beat down, and they'd need more breaks.

For a long time, the girls hiked in silence. Cora was thinking about Lucas. How she made him lie to their mom about this trip.

"What are you thinking about?" Rayna asked after a while.

"Lucas," Cora said. "For making him lie. Do you think he'll forgive me?"

"I don't know," Rayna said. "He's very upset. But he has other things on his mind. Like Lena being pregnant."

"He told you?"

"Yeah. He's so scared."

Cora imagined Lucas taking care of a baby. He would

make a great dad. But he wanted to go to college. It would be hard to do both. But if anyone could do it, it was Lucas.

"If they do have a baby, I'm going to help them. I'll be the best aunt ever."

Rayna nodded. "Aunt Cora. I can totally see it."

Chapter 19

Treasured Times

Cora and Rayna continued on the trail. The visitor's lot was about two miles away. They walked in silence until Cora spotted something. She stopped.

"Rayna! Look!" She was pointing to something just off the path. It was lying in some weeds.

"What is it?" Rayna asked. She went over to look. "Ew! A dead rabbit. Its guts are hanging out."

"Yeah, but look at the bird."

"It's eating the rabbit. I don't want to see that."

Cora stepped closer. "It's a condor."

"Be careful," Rayna said. "Don't get too close."

The bird spread its wings.

"Wow!" Cora said. "Look at that wingspan. It must be eight feet! I have to take a picture for Lucas."

She was about to reach for her camera. But it was too

late. The bird flew away. The girls stood watching until it was gone.

"Come on," Rayna said.

"Just a sec." Cora was looking over at the weeds again. Something was on the ground. She went over and picked it up. "A condor feather," she said.

"Cool," Rayna said. "You found a treasure after all."

"Come on. Let's go!" Cora was suddenly in a hurry. She smiled at the feather in her hand. She couldn't wait to show her brother.

The girls walked in silence. They had a good pace going. Their strides were long and steady. They were ready for this hike to be over.

When they got to the lot, Rayna called her dad for a ride. It would be a while until he got there.

"Look at us," Rayna said. "We're covered in dirt."

"And I smell bad," Cora said.

Rayna laughed. "I think I smell even worse."

"You were quiet on the trail," Cora said. "What were you thinking about?"

"What I'm going to do with my summer," Rayna said.

"Camp all summer long?" Cora said. She gave Rayna a little smile.

"Not quite," Rayna said.

Cora didn't say anything.

"That's it?" Rayna said after a minute. "You're giving up already? I was sure you'd try to talk me into it."

"You mean you'd do it?"

"Maybe one or two trips," Rayna said. She paused. "Do you ever imagine yourself in the future?"

"That's all I've been doing for two days. I see myself hiking and camping for sure. And I'd like a job that's outdoors. What about you?"

"I want to help people," Rayna said. "As we were walking, I saw myself speaking out on issues. People were inspired by what I said." She smiled as she spoke. "I want to be part of something powerful. Something that makes the world better."

Tears filled Cora's eyes. It was hard to hear Rayna's ideas about the future. They were so different from her own. Would they continue to be friends? She quickly wiped the tears away.

"You will," Cora said. "You're kind and smart and honest. People will listen to you. You will be able to make change happen."

"Thanks, Cora. You're a good friend."

About an hour later, Rayna's dad pulled into the lot and parked. He helped the girls load their packs.

"Wait," Cora said. "Before we go. I have to get a selfie of us."

"You? Taking a selfie?" Rayna said.

"People change," Cora said. "A good friend told me that."

Rayna looked down. "I was hard on you. I'm sorry."

Cora put her arm around her best friend. "Smile," Cora said as she held up her phone.

The girls leaned toward each other. Cora took the picture. She knew she would treasure it forever.

Chapter 20

Looking Forward

Rayna's dad pulled up in front of Cora's house. Lucas's truck was in the driveway. What would she say to him? Would he even listen?

She thanked Rayna's dad for the ride. "I'll text you later," she said to Rayna. She got out of the car and went inside. The house was quiet. Maybe Lucas was out jogging. That would give her time to clean up before they talked.

Then Cora heard a sound. It was coming from the kitchen. A few seconds later, Lucas came out.

"Lucas—" She didn't have a chance to finish.

"Cora!" He ran over and hugged her. Then he picked her up like he did when she was little.

"I've been so worried. I should have gone with you. I'm sorry."

"No!" she said. "You shouldn't be sorry. *I'm* sorry. For being selfish. And for making you lie to Mom."

"I didn't lie," Lucas said.

"What do you mean?"

"Well, at first I lied. But then Rayna and I talked. She said she was going after you. So I called Mom and told her everything. She'll be home soon."

"Did you tell her about Lena?" Cora asked.

"Yeah. But it's okay. Lena finally took a test. She's not pregnant. We both feel better. It's too soon to have a baby."

"Is Mom mad at me?" Cora asked.

"She's not happy. She'll be happier when she sees you're okay. But Mom also knows how you love the outdoors. How inspired you get by nature. It makes her happy to see you happy. But don't do it again! You should always have someone with you."

Cora thought back to when she'd gotten lost. Then she'd fallen. It could have been much worse.

"You're right," she said.

"So," Lucas said. "Tell me about it. Did you make it to Summer Lake?"

"We did. It was a big sandy pit. With green, smelly slime at the bottom."

"But did you find treasure?" Lucas asked.

"Oh!" she said. "That's right. The treasure. It's in my pack."

"What did you find? Gold coins?"

Cora smiled. "Something much better." She pulled the feather from the pack.

"Oh wow!" he said. "Is that what I think it is?"

"Yep."

Lucas picked up the feather. He ran his fingers along the vane. "It's from a condor. Did you see one? Alive?"

"Yes," Cora said. "Rayna and I got a good look at it. It was huge."

"That's so amazing," Lucas said. "I wish I'd been there."

"Me too. But at least you have the feather."

"Thanks. And good job on the hike. I'll admit I was mad that you did it. But I'm proud of you."

That's what she was hoping to hear. "I have more to tell you," she said. "But first I want to take a shower."

"Real quick. Did you and Rayna make up?"

"We talked a lot. And we agreed on one thing. Both of us made mistakes. I wish I could do it all again. I'd be a better listener."

"You seem a little sad," he said.

"Rayna and I are so different. I don't think she wants to hike the PCT anymore. I'd be sad to lose her."

"Why would you lose her? You care so much about each other."

"But Rayna has big dreams. She wants to change the world. I just want to be out in nature."

"You have dreams and goals too. They're just as good. And who says you can't be friends? I have friends who live far away. We hardly ever see each other. But when we do, it's like old times. You might have to work at it a little. But Rayna is worth it."

"You're so smart, Lucas."

"So are you. For a kid." He smiled. "I'll tell you what. If Rayna can't do the hike with you, I will. Go get cleaned up. I'll make you something to eat. Mac and cheese?"

"Yes, please." Cora went to her room. She looked at the selfie of her and Rayna. They looked tired and sweaty. Their clothes were filthy. But they looked happy.

"I want to post some pictures. Can U help me?" Cora texted.

"Be there in a few," Rayna texted back. "We can talk about the PCT."

Cora grinned. Rayna was still thinking about the Pacific Crest Trail hike! She thought about what Lucas had said. There was a bond between true friends. It was that way with Cora and Rayna. No matter where their paths might lead them, their friendship would last.

WANT TO KEEP READING?

9781680214765

Turn the page for a sneak peek
at another book in the Monarch
Jungle series.

Chapter 1

Sun and Shadows

Ask me my favorite sport. I'd have to say kayaking. It's good exercise. And it's a mental workout too. There's something about facing the elements. It tests every part of you. Sunny weather is a bonus. But this is Saddle City. Chances of sun in the mountains are fifty-fifty.

It was just after sunrise. I rode with my dad. Two kayaks were in the back of his pickup. My best friend, Juan, was in his truck. He followed us to a fishing site. That's where he left his truck. Then we drove on to the launch site. From here, Juan and I would paddle back.

My dad helped us unload the kayaks. Then we slid them into the water and got in. Our 15-mile ride started now. We waved back at my dad and started paddling.

Juan and I had been here before. We knew Blackwater River well. It was broken up into sections. The upper part was mostly flat. The water was calm. Earlier I'd checked the forecast. So far it was in my favor.

A few minutes had gone by. I looked up at the sky. There were a few gray patches. Though I was no expert, I knew clouds. These led to rain. So much for the forecast.

The rest of the sky was blue. We'd be fine, I told myself. But one thought nagged at me. Clouds don't lie.

"Let's pick up the pace." I pointed up with my paddle. "See those clouds? We need to get ahead of them."

Juan was eating an energy bar. "Wait, don't tell me. They spoke to you." He laughed so hard, bits of food flew from his mouth.

"Keep your mouth shut, fool. Remember who you're talking to."

"So sorry, Cloud Warrior. But I say you're wrong. Those clouds look harmless." Juan laughed.

"Go ahead. Laugh. I'll enjoy seeing that smirk wiped off your face."

Juan jabbed his middle finger at me. "Whatever." He took off paddling.

I surged toward him. "What's with you?"

"What do you mean? I'm being my usual charming self. It's why the babes drool over me."

"Rabid dogs drool over you."

"I have my admirers." A zit on his nose shone in the sun.

"Have you looked in a mirror? We're not exactly sex symbols."

"Speak for yourself," Juan said.

I was. Most girls in my class towered over me. I wore glasses. My ears stuck out. And I was already losing my hair.

Our look was not high fashion. At school, we wore whatever was clean. On the water, we looked really sloppy. Wide-brimmed hats. Ragged shorts and T-shirts. Our life vests had some style. But we'd end up covered in mud anyway.

The kayaks didn't look so good either. Mine had bird poop on it. It was baked on by the sun. Juan's had oil splatters from working on his truck.

We weren't cool. But we were prepared. Our dry bags carried supplies. Rope. Flashlights. First-aid kit. Extra clothes. Water and snacks.

Juan's paddle sliced the water in rhythm with mine.

"It's getting hot," Juan said. He pushed up his sleeves.

Normally we wouldn't be sweating this soon. But the air was so dry. Another sign of a storm. "It won't last," I told Juan. "We just have to get ahead of the weather." I wasn't going to let anything ruin this trip.